Dear Parents and Educators,

Welcome to Penguin Young Readers! As parents and educators, you
know that each child develops at his or her own pace—in terms of
speech, critical thinking, and, of course, reading. Penguin Young
Readers recognizes this fact. As a result, each Penguin Young Readers
book is assigned a traditional easy-to-read level (1–4) as well as a
Guided Reading Level (A–P). Both of these systems will help you choose
the right book for your child. Please refer to the back of each book
for specific leveling information. Penguin Young Readers features
esteemed authors and illustrators, stories about favorite characters,
fascinating nonfiction, and more!

Batman: The Brave and the Bold Batman and Friends	LEVEL **2**
	GUIDED READING LEVEL **I**

This book is perfect for a **Progressing Reader** who:
- can figure out unknown words by using picture and context clues;
- can recognize beginning, middle, and ending sounds;
- can make and confirm predictions about what will happen in the text; and
- can distinguish between fiction and nonfiction.

Here are some **activities** you can do during and after reading this book:
- Compare/Contrast: Batman and his friends are super heroes, but they all
  have different powers and personalities. On a separate sheet of paper,
  write down the names of Batman's friends and a few words that describe
  each of them. How are they alike? How are they different?
- Retelling: While fighting crime, Batman and his friends have a lot of
  wild adventures together. Pick one adventure mentioned in the story and
  discuss what happened. How did Batman and his friends work as a team?
- Make Connections: Batman always makes sure to thank his friends for all
  their help. Can you think of a time when your friends helped you? How
  did you say thanks?

Remember, sharing the love of reading with a child is the best gift
you can give!

—Bonnie Bader, EdM
  Penguin Young Readers program

*Penguin Young Readers are leveled by independent reviewers applying the standards developed by Irene Fountas
and Gay Su Pinnell in *Matching Books to Readers: Using Leveled Books in Guided Reading*, Heinemann, 1999.

Penguin Young Readers
Published by the Penguin Group
Penguin Group (USA) Inc., 375 Hudson Street, New York, New York 10014, USA
Penguin Group (Canada), 90 Eglinton Avenue East, Suite 700,
Toronto, Ontario M4P 2Y3, Canada
(a division of Pearson Penguin Canada Inc.)
Penguin Books Ltd., 80 Strand, London WC2R 0RL, England
Penguin Group Ireland, 25 St. Stephen's Green, Dublin 2, Ireland
(a division of Penguin Books Ltd.)
Penguin Group (Australia), 250 Camberwell Road, Camberwell, Victoria 3124, Australia
(a division of Pearson Australia Group Pty. Ltd.)
Penguin Books India Pvt. Ltd., 11 Community Centre, Panchsheel Park,
New Delhi—110 017, India
Penguin Group (NZ), 67 Apollo Drive, Rosedale, Auckland 0632, New Zealand
(a division of Pearson New Zealand Ltd.)
Penguin Books (South Africa) (Pty.) Ltd., 24 Sturdee Avenue,
Rosebank, Johannesburg 2196, South Africa

Penguin Books Ltd., Registered Offices: 80 Strand, London WC2R 0RL, England

Published by Penguin Young Readers, an imprint of Penguin Group (USA) Inc., 345 Hudson Street,
New York, New York 10014. Manufactured in China.

ISBN 978-0-448-45870-0   10 9 8 7 6 5 4 3 2 1

PENGUIN YOUNG READERS

Level 2

PROGRESSING READER

adapted by Jade Ashe
based on teleplays by J. M. DeMatteis, Marsha Griffin,
and Steven Melching
Batman created by Bob Kane

Penguin Young Readers
An Imprint of Penguin Group (USA) Inc.

Batman is one of the greatest super heroes of all time.

Sometimes he has to team up with other heroes to get a tough job done.

It is a good thing he has so many friends to choose from.

One of his best friends

is Aquaman.

Together they have lots of

adventures under the sea.

Once they had to stop Aquaman's
evil brother from taking over
the ocean.

It is a good thing Aquaman

was there.

He is a much better swimmer

than Batman.

Together the two friends stopped
Aquaman's brother and saved
the ocean.

Batman is also friends with
all the Green Lanterns.
Once he was even asked
to join them.

A scary alien was trying to take over, and Batman needed to call on some powerful friends to help.

It is a good thing he wasn't

by himself.

This alien was pretty tough.

Batman makes sure to always thank his friends for their help.

He also has a friend named

Plastic Man.

Together they always have

wild adventures.

One time they came across

a real, live dinosaur.

It was big enough to eat both

of them.

Even Batman knows that sometimes it is okay to run away from a fight.

Gorilla Grodd is a lot worse than a giant dinosaur.

He is also smarter than he looks.

Once he even turned Batman

into a gorilla just like him.

It is a good thing Batman's
friend Plastic Man was there
to help.

Another one of Batman's good
friends is Green Arrow.

One of their wildest adventures was when a wizard sent them back in time.

A witch used a magic spell to turn Batman into a dark knight.

The magic made Batman fight

his friend.

That is something he would

never do.

It is a good thing that the power of friendship is stronger than any magic spell.

Together Batman and
Green Arrow made the
wizard send them home.

When Robin was little, he and the other young heroes got into all kinds of trouble.

Sometimes he would even go out and try to stop the bad guys on his own.

Even after they grew up, Robin, Aqualad, and Speedy stayed the best of friends.

They even found new ways to get
into trouble.

It is a good thing they could count on Batman and his friends to show up and save the day.

Batman taught Robin and his friends about teamwork.

With all his amazing friends, Batman never has to worry about fighting crime alone.